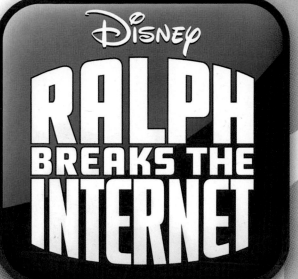

Disney

RALPH
BREAKS THE
INTERNET

Look and Find®

we make books come alive™

pi kids® **Phoenix International Publications, Inc.**

Chicago • London • New York • Hamburg • Mexico City • Paris • Sydney

BEEP-BEEP-BEEP! That sound means a new game has been plugged in at Litwak's arcade! Vanellope von Schweetz hopes it's a new racing game—she knows all the tracks in *Sugar Rush* by heart. But *WiFi* isn't a game, it's the Internet...whatever that is.

While Wreck-It Ralph tries to pronounce *WiFi*, say hello to these characters from all over the arcade:

 Calhoun

 Zombie

 Vanellope

 Sour Bill

 Gene

 Surge

 Felix

 Ralph

Vanellope's game, *Sugar Rush*, needs a new steering wheel. The only place to get one is from eBay. Ralph and Vanellope are going to the Internet! On the busy Internet streets, they look for someone who can give them directions. KnowsMore seems like a helpful fellow!

this pop-up

cookies

recycle bin

KnowsMore

this pop-up

e-mail truck

The highest dollar item on Spamley's list is Shank's car from *Slaughter Race*. The game is a shark-eat-dog world of missile explosions, trash fires, and creepy clowns. Vanellope feels like she has found a new home! Ralph, on the other hand, is ready to go back to Litwak's.

Help Ralph and Vanellope sneak around Shank and her gang:

Felony

Pyro

Debbie

Butcher Boy

Shank

Litwak's Family Fun Center is home to arcade games, old and new. Head back to Game Central Station and collect these game items—no quarters required!

mug of root beer

potion

coin

cherries

wooden sword

turkey leg

key

security

HTML construction worker

e-mail carrier

finder

recycler

pop-up blocker

Do I hear three-and-a-quarter? Click back to eBay and try to outbid these "players":

Need to make a little moola? Meander back to Spamley's and grab these fliers:

There's no place like *Slaughter Race!* Throw it in reverse and steer around these unique *Slaughter Race* things:

stolen refrigerator

clown

sewer shark

this mace

pigeon

this car

trash fire

Race back to Felix and Calhoun's apartment and find 20 medals from *Fix-It Felix, Jr.*

FELIX

It's Caturday! Browse back to BuzzzTube and find videos starring these photogenic felines:

Some of the Ralph copies didn't turn out quite right. Return to the clones and find these irregular Ralphs:

Congratulations, you've unlocked the bonus level! Go back and find a plate of pancakes and a milkshake in each scene.